SandCastle 2

More Blends

ph

Carey Molter

ABDO
Publishing Company

Published by SandCastle™, an imprint of ABDO Publishing Company, 4940 Viking Drive, Edina, Minnesota 55435.

Printed in the United States.

Cover and interior photo credits: Artville, Corbis Images, Image 100, PhotoDisc, PictureQuest, Rubberball Productions.

Library of Congress Cataloging-in-Publication Data

Molter, Carey, 1973-
    Ph / Molter Carey.
      p. cm. -- (Blends)
    ISBN 1-57765-451-X
    1. Readers (Primary) [1. Readers.] I. Title. II. Blends (Series)

    PE1119 .M63 2000
    428.1--dc21

00-056561

The SandCastle concept, content, and reading method have been reviewed and approved by a national advisory board including literacy specialists, librarians, elementary school teachers, early childhood education professionals, and parents.

Let Us Know

After reading the book, SandCastle would like you to tell us your stories about reading. What is your favorite page? Was there something hard that you needed help with? Share the ups and downs of learning to read. We want to hear from you! To get posted on the ABDO Publishing Company Web site, send us email at:

sandcastle@abdopub.com

Second printing 2002

About SandCastle™

Nonfiction books for the beginning reader

- Basic concepts of phonics are incorporated with integrated language methods of reading instruction. Most words are short, and phrases, letter sounds, and word sounds are repeated.

- Readability is determined by the number of words in each sentence, the number of characters in each word, and word lists based on curriculum frameworks.

- Full-color photography reinforces word meanings and concepts.

- "Words I Can Read" list at the end of each book teaches basic elements of grammar, helps the reader recognize the words in the text, and builds vocabulary.

- Reading levels are indicated by the number of flags on the castle.

Look for more SandCastle books in these three reading levels:

Level 1
(one flag)

Grades Pre-K to K
5 or fewer words per page

Level 2
(two flags)

Grades K to 1
5 to 10 words per page

Level 3
(three flags)

Grades 1 to 2
10 to 15 words per page

ph

Phil has fun with his sister.

Her name is Josephine.

ph

Phila likes to pet the dolphin.

ph

Phillip plays with his alphabet game.

ph

Ralph likes talking on
the phone.

11

ph

Sophia wears headphones to play a game at school.

ph

Sophie yells into this megaphone.

It makes her voice loud.

ph

This kitten is an orphan.

Steph will take it home.

ph

Stephen likes to take photos.

ph

What did Stephi win?

(trophies)

Words I Can Read

Nouns

A noun is a person, place, or thing

dolphin (DOL-fin) p. 7
fun (FUHN) p. 5
game (GAME) pp. 9, 13
headphones (HED-fohnz) p. 13
home (HOME) p. 17
kitten (KIT-uhn) p. 17
megaphone (MEG-uh-fohn) p. 15

name (NAYM) p. 5
orphan (OR-fuhn) p. 17
phone (FOHN) p. 11
school (SKOOL) p. 13
sister (SISS-ter) p. 5
voice (VOISS) p. 15

Plural Nouns

A plural noun is more than one person, place, or thing

photos (FOH-tohs) p. 19   **trophies** (TROH-feez) p. 21

Proper Nouns

A proper noun is the name of a person, place, or thing

Josephine (JOH-se-feen) p. 5
Phil (FIL) p. 5

Phila (FIL-uh) p. 7
Phillip (FIL-uhp) p. 9
Ralph (RALF) p. 11

Sophia (so-FEE-ya) p. 13
Sophie (SO-fee) p. 15
Steph (STEF) p. 17

Stephen (STEEF-uhn) p. 19
Stephi (STEF-ee) p. 21

Verbs

A verb is an action or being word

has (HAZ) p. 5
is (IZ) pp. 5, 17
likes (LIKESS) pp. 7, 11, 19
makes (MAKESS) p. 15
pet (PET) p. 7
play (PLAY) p. 13
plays (PLAYZ) p. 9

take (TAYK) pp. 17, 19
talking (TAWK-ing) p. 11
wears (WAIRZ) p. 13
will (WIL) p. 17
win (WIN) p. 21
yells (YELZ) p. 15

Adjectives

An adjective describes something

alphabet (AL-fuh-bet) p. 9
her (HUR) pp. 5, 15
his (HIZ) pp. 5, 9

loud (LOUD) p. 15
this (THISS) pp. 15, 17

Match these ph Words
to the Pictures

trophy

megaphone

dolphin

gophers